THIS BOOK BELONGS TO

....

RUMPELSTILTSKIN

Written by Helen Anderton

Illustrated by Stuart Lynch

make
believe
ideas

Reading together

This book is designed to be fun for children who are gaining confidence in their reading. They will enjoy and benefit from some time discussing the story with an adult. Here are some ways you can help your child take those first steps in reading:

❀ Encourage your child to look at the pictures and talk about what is happening in the story.

❀ Help your child to find familiar words and sound out the letters in harder words.

❀ Ask your child to read and repeat each short sentence.

Look at rhymes

Many of the sentences in this book are simple rhymes. Encourage your child to recognise rhyming words. Try asking the following questions:

❀ What does this word say?

❀ Can you find a word that rhymes with it?

❀ Look at the ending of two words that rhyme. Are they spelt the same? For example, "green" and "queen", and "said" and "thread".

Reading activities

The **What happens next?** activity encourages your child to retell the story and point to the mixed-up pictures in the right order.

The **Rhyming words** activity takes six words from the story and asks your child to read and find other words that rhyme with them.

The **Key words** pages provide practice with common words used in the context of the book. Read the sentences with your child and encourage him or her to make up more sentences using the key words listed around the border.

A **Picture dictionary** page asks children to focus closely on nine words from the story. Encourage your child to look carefully at each word, cover it with his or her hand, write it on a separate piece of paper, and finally, check it!

Do not complete all the activities at once – doing one each time you read will ensure that your child continues to enjoy the story and the time you are spending together. Have fun!

King Stan lived on a mountaintop
    where winter didn't seem to stop.
"I'm so alone - and bored, " Stan cried,
    "I'm off to find myself a bride!"

One day while searching for his queen,
     Stan met the miller's girl, Maureen.
"My girl's different," the miller said.
     "She spins straw into golden thread."

"Wow!" said Stan, "I'm so impressed!
     Let's prove this with a spinning test."
So in a room piled high with straw,
     he left Maureen and locked the door.

9

"What can I do?" poor Maureen cried.

"I can't spin gold! My father lied."

Then, suddenly, out from the straw

a voice called: "Hey! I'll help, for sure."

And in a flash of purple smoke,
first she saw a golden cloak,
then two shoes in gold and cream,
and the smallest man you've ever seen!

"I'll spin gold – but not for free.

Your ring will be my pay," said he.

"Ok," sighed Maureen, "please begin."

And the little man sat down to spin.

Stan was thrilled but wanted more;
next he filled THREE rooms with straw!

So with fine jewels and hats with frills,
Maureen paid her spinning bills.

The man kept spinning as before
until Maureen could pay no more.
Said he, "Give me your firstborn son!"
In tears, she said, "The deal is done."

At last, Maureen became the queen!

(Stan's suit was gold, but she wore green.)

Soon they had a baby boy,

who filled their lives with love and joy.

A year had passed when one cold day,
    the man came back to fetch his pay.
Maureen cried, "Please take my jewels!"
    Said he, "Dear girl, you knew the rules."

She said, "Is there no other way?
    I promise, I'll do what you say!"
"Ok," he said, "let's play a game;
    you're free if you can guess my name."

Maureen's servants searched all week,
'til singing on a snowy peak
they heard: "The queen will never win.
For who would guess Rum-pel-stilt-skin?"

The man returned that very night
and sneered, "You'll never get it right!"
So Maureen said, "What can it be?
Perhaps it's George or Bill or Lee?"

"Or one that's better than the rest?
Yes, RUMPELSTILTSKIN, that's my guess!"

In rage, the man flew out the door!
And Maureen was free forever more.

What happens next?

Some of the pictures from the story have been mixed up! Can you retell the story and point to each picture in the correct order?

Rhyming words

Read the words in the middle of each group and point to the other words that rhyme with them.

cried

bride

day

ride

spin

baby

came

game

name

queen

pay

say

day

straw

three

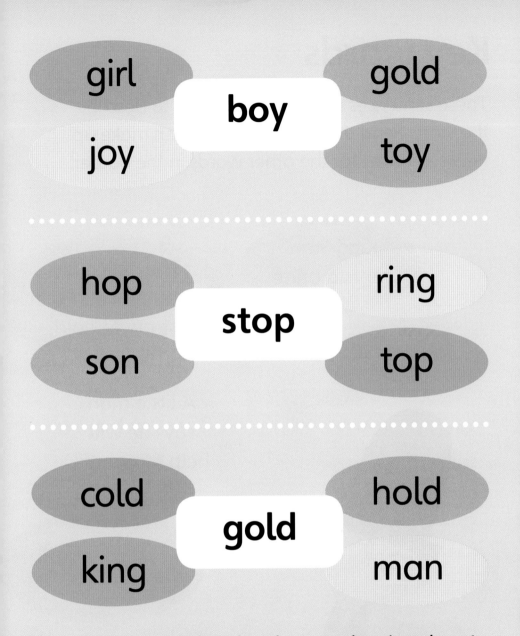

girl

boy

gold

joy

toy

hop

stop

ring

son

top

cold

gold

hold

king

man

Now choose a word and make up a rhyming chant!

I **hold gold** when I am **cold!**

Key words

These sentences use common words to describe the story. Read the sentences and then make up new sentences for the other words in the border.

King Stan wants **a** bride.

The miller says Maureen **can** spin straw to gold.

A little man says he **will** help Maureen.

Maureen gives the man **her** ring.

Maureen can't pay **for** the gold.

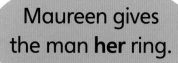

look · very

· his · but · with · day · an · can · we · are · up · had ·

She says she will give the man her son.

When Maureen is queen, she has a baby.

The man tells Maureen to guess **his** name.

Maureen's servants **look** for the man.

Maureen says the name **and** the man goes away.

the · a · and · to · see · in · was · I · will · it · he · you · of · she · on · for · when

my · her · is · there · out · at · then · have · so · be ·

Picture dictionary

Look carefully at the pictures and the words.
Now cover the words, one at a time.
Can you remember how to write them?

bride

cloak

jewels

miller

peak

servants

straw

suit

thread